# Marilyn's Monster

# Marilyn's Monster

MICHELLE KNUDSEN     illustrated by MATT PHELAN

WALKER BOOKS
AND SUBSIDIARIES
LONDON · BOSTON · SYDNEY · AUCKLAND

Some of the kids in Marilyn's class had monsters.
It was the latest thing. Marilyn didn't have a monster.
Not yet. You couldn't just go out and get one.
Your monster had to find you.
That was just the way it worked.

Some kids woke up to find their
monsters had chosen them
while they slept.

Some kids got their monsters
on the way home from school.
Or on the bus.
Or in the park.

Timmy's monster chose him right
in the middle of a history test.

At first Marilyn wasn't even worried about it. Eventually her
monster would find her, too. There were still a bunch of kids
who didn't have monsters yet.

But then Franklin got his at the library.

And Rebecca got hers while she was riding her bike.

And Lenny got his while he was running away from some mean older kids who kept picking on him.

Nobody picked on Lenny
any more after that.

After a while, Marilyn was the only one left without a monster. She knew she wasn't supposed to try to look for him. But she kind of did anyway. She hung around the library, hoping.

She poked around the playground, pretending not to look under the slide and behind the climbing bars. She watched the others with their monsters, playing and laughing and having fun and never being alone.

At night, when her room was dark and scary, Marilyn thought about how good it would be to have her monster there beside her.

"We're sure you'll get your monster soon," said her parents.

"I bet you'll never get one," said her brother.
"It probably came already and took one look
at you and ran the other way."

Marilyn tried to be patient. She tried to believe her monster was still coming. She made sure she brushed her hair very carefully every morning and wore pretty clothes and smiled a lot and tried to look very friendly and interesting and clever and fun to be around. She tried to be the kind of girl no monster could resist.

But at the end of the week, her monster still hadn't come.
She was afraid that maybe her brother was right.

"Maybe I'm better off without a monster," she told her friend Deborah at school. "They seem like a lot of work."

"Hmm," said Deborah. She didn't really seem to agree.

"Maybe your monster's just running late," said Margaret.

"Maybe it's invisible, and it's been here all along and you didn't even notice," said Jerome.

That night in her room, Marilyn whispered into the scary dark.

"Are you invisible? Have you really been here all along?"

But if her monster was there, he didn't say so.

Marilyn stopped trying to seem pretty and nice and friendly
and fun all the time. She stopped looking around in the library
and the playground after school. She started feeling cross.
Where was her monster?
What was taking him so long?

She was so cross, sometimes she thought maybe she
really *didn't* want a monster. What was so great about
monsters anyway?

But they were pretty great. She could see that they were.
She wanted one more than she could say.

"That's it," Marilyn said one morning. "I'm going to find my monster."

"You can't," said her brother. "That's not the way it works."

"Maybe," said Marilyn. "But you don't really know. Maybe my monster is different."

She put on her good walking shoes and packed a thermos of juice and a peanut-butter and banana sandwich. Then she made a second sandwich and put that in her bag, too.

Marilyn went out and started looking.
She didn't just *kind of* look. She *really* looked.
She looked as hard as she could.
She searched behind the stone lions
that sat outside the library.

She checked beneath the
benches at the playground
and in the park.

She went down the winding path through the woods
and out into the big field with the wild flowers.
She didn't see her monster.

Marilyn stopped in the middle of the field. She closed her eyes and stood very still. She thought about trying to sing a beautiful song like the ones those princesses in films sometimes sang that made all the little animals come and sit on their shoulders. She thought about trying again to be patient and wait and hope that her monster would find her one day soon. Then she took a deep, deep breath and shouted in her loudest, loudest voice.

And then, very softly, she heard a voice say, "Here."

Marilyn followed the voice. It was very quiet, but she could hear it very clearly. She followed it across the field and into the woods on the other side and over to a tall, tall tree.

And there was her monster, half hidden among the leaves.

"I got lost," her monster said in his small, soft voice.
"And then I got scared. And then I got stuck."

Her monster had two long, lovely wings. They were
tangled and caught in the branches.

Marilyn climbed up and, very gently, helped her monster get free.

"I kept hoping you would come and find me," her monster said.

"I'm sorry it took me so long," Marilyn said back.

Then they sat there together and had peanut-butter and banana sandwiches and juice.

When they were ready, Marilyn's monster lifted her up
and flew her all the way back home.

"Oh, sweetie!" said her parents. "Your monster found you at last!"

"We found each other," Marilyn said.
She and her monster smiled together.

"It's not supposed to work that way," her brother said.

Marilyn just looked at him. She didn't think he was right about that. She thought there were a lot of different ways that things could work.

And that night when Marilyn went to bed, the dark didn't seem so scary. Marilyn wasn't sad, or afraid, or lonely. She was happy.

Marilyn's monster was, too.

*For some of my favourite friends:*
*Emily, Alex, Maddie, Sophie, Evie and Tommy*

M. K.

*To all the amazing friends I've found or who have found me*

M. P.

First published 2015 by Walker Books Ltd
87 Vauxhall Walk, London SE11 5HJ

2 4 6 8 10 9 7 5 3 1

Text © 2015 Michelle Knudsen
Illustrations © 20125 Matt Phelan

The right of Michelle Knudsen and Matt Phelan to be identified as author and illustrator respectively
of this work has been asserted by them in accordance with the Copyright, Designs and Patents Act 1988

This book has been typeset in Kennerly

Printed in China

British Library Cataloguing in Publication Data:
a catalogue record for this book is available from the British Library

ISBN 978-1-4063-6194-0

www.walker.co.uk